BUTTERFLY BOY

Additional Titles by Mary Hiker

Good Friends
Play Fetch
Strange Outfit
Underwater

BUTTERFLY BOY

AN AVERY BARKS DOG MYSTERY

Mary Hiker

This is a work of fiction. Names, characters, places, and incidents are a product of the author's imagination. Locales and public names are sometimes used for atmospheric purposes. Any resemblance to actual people, living or dead, or to businesses, companies, events, institutions, or locales is completely coincidental.

Printed in the United States of America
Second Printing, 2015

Butterfly Boy - Mary Hiker – 2nd ed.

ISBN-13:978-1518629082
ISBN-10:1518629083

Published By Awesome Dog

www.MaryHiker.com

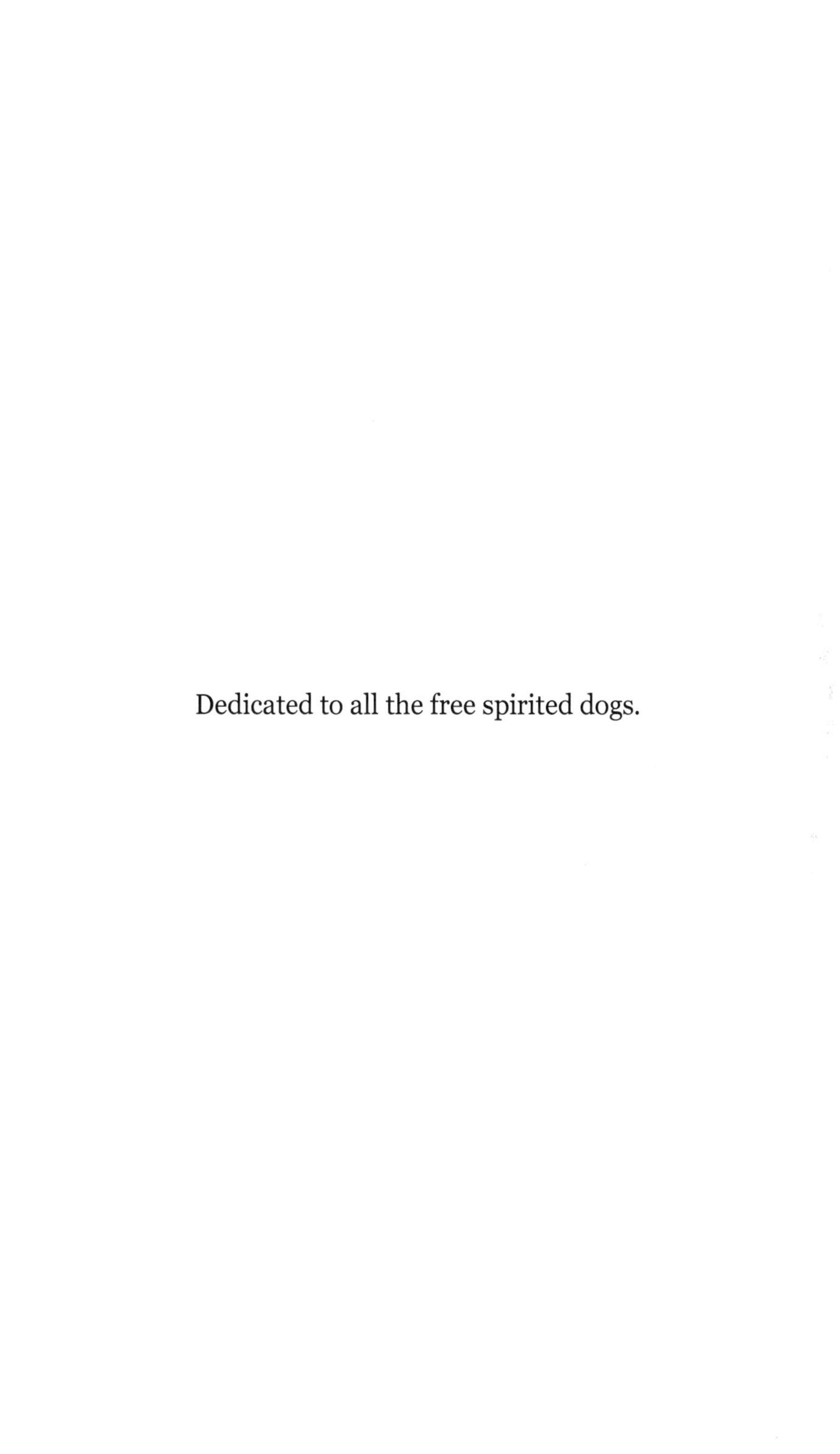

Dedicated to all the free spirited dogs.

Chapter 1

"They were out here again trying to get my babies!"

Miss Judy grabbed on to me so tightly that her fingernails dug into my arm. For a lady in her eighties, she sure had a lot of grip strength. Her gray hair flew all over the place and she was almost out of breath. Jase Johnson and his buddies had trespassed on her land, hunting 'her' deer again.

I regularly stopped by to check in on Miss Judy since her husband died last year. This time, I found her sobbing and borderline hysterical. She was an animal lover and regarded the deer - and other wildlife - on her land as family.

"Will you take your dog and make them go away?" she asked with tears in her eyes.

She didn't realize that my golden retriever, Chevy, would never scare anyone, especially the likes of Jase and his buddies. That is, unless they were afraid of getting licked to death.

But, if it meant easing her mind and letting Chevy run and play on her land, I was happy to help, my volunteer work is to find people after all. Miss Judy lived on over seven hundred acres that had been handed down to her through the generations. It had a nice mix of woods and pasture, and some of the most beautiful views the mountains of western North Carolina had to offer.

Besides, I reasoned, it was already past noon, and the hunters would be out of the woods by now. Well, I hoped they would be out of the woods. Being alone out there with a bunch of bullies with guns was not my idea of fun. It was way outside the scope of my training.

I turned to my dog. “Hey Chevy, wanna go hike?”

Chevy picked up his leash and shook his head back and forth as fast as it would go. He loved whipping his leash all around in the air like that. He was so excited, it even made Miss Judy smile.

“Thank you, Chevy, you are my hero,” she said, still trembling with fear and rage.

I headed out behind her little farm house with my dog. Chevy trotted along, enjoying all the sights and smells of nature. He lived his life happy, and was just plain grateful to have a home and someone to love him.

We walked along the edge of a pasture and down a dirt road through Miss Judy’s woods, my hiking boots kicking up small wisps of dust as Chevy’s pads landed softly on the loose soil. First stop was the spot where I had posted some “No Hunting” signs the week before.

About a quarter mile from the house, I glanced up toward the trees and my stomach immediately tightened. My “No Hunting” signs were covered in bullet holes. One sign even had “JASE was HERE” written in black marker, right on top of the words “No

Hunting". There were shotgun shells and empty cigarette boxes scattered all over the grass. Jase and his friends had trespassed, all right, and they didn't care who knew it.

The distant hum of an engine wafted over the trees, and grew into a loud rumble. A truck was coming up the dirt road, fast. I didn't want any trouble from Jase and his boys, so I grabbed Chevy's collar and ducked into the woods. We quickly crouched down behind a fallen tree, as a huge black truck with oversized tires roared past. It spewed up dirt as it fishtailed around a curve.

A deep, gravelly voice hollered out as the truck flew by, "Just try to stop us, Nature Girl!"

How did they see me? I wondered.

I stood and brushed the leaves and debris off my knees, deciding it was a good time to get out of the immediate area. I cut back through the woods and stayed off the dirt road to avoid a confrontation with the hooligans.

My plan was to follow the narrow creek that lead back to a paved country road at the edge of Miss Judy's property. That road led back to her home and my truck. Better safe than sorry. Those guys had guns, were highly arrogant and half crazy.

It was definitely time to get the law involved in this.

My heart beat hard like a drum and my shoulders tensed as we made our way through the woods. I constantly looked over my shoulder and kept up a good pace the entire journey. The vegetation was still soaked from the previous night's rain, and wet leaves slapped my face as I trudged through the underbrush.

Meanwhile, Chevy played in the creek and seemed oblivious to any kind of trouble.

My boots were covered with mud and my pants were wet by the time we popped out of the woods and into a large field. As we left the cover of the trees, sunshine replaced the shade. Tension started to leave my body as the sun warmed my shoulders and the old country road appeared off in the distance.

Chevy discovered some purple butterflies fluttering around the edge of the field and romped over to investigate. He was completely captivated as his new friends flittered around his head.

I brushed the hair that had escaped from my ponytail from my face and continued moving across the field toward the paved road. Chevy would catch up to me when he was ready. The sooner we got back to my truck at Miss Judy's place, the better. It was time to get some help dealing with Jase and his crew.

As I walked, a dark mound came into focus on the ground up ahead of me. I couldn't figure out what it was from a distance, and headed over in that direction to take a closer look. As I approached the object, a familiar humming sound filled the air all around me. The noise grew louder and more intense as I got closer to the mound.

I should have ignored it. I should have walked around it. But curiosity got the best of me and I went over to take a look.

As I approached, hundreds of flies buzzed back and forth and landed on the object. Then reality hit me. It was a human body, crumpled up and lying in this field right in front of me. He wore dark colored clothes with a patch on the shoulder of his black jacket. The flies landed on a wound on the side of the man's head and his slicked back hair was mixed with blood.

I took a shallow breath and noticed there wasn't a strong smell. The death must have been fairly recent. No matter how many dead bodies I've seen, I've never gotten used to it. I glanced up to check on my dog. He was still bounding around playing with butterflies about fifty yards away.

My focus slowly returned to the body lying in front of me. Gradually, I recognized the dark jacket with the red and white bulls-eye patch. I purposely slowed my breathing, then bent over and looked at the dead guy's face.

Oh no, I recognized the stranger. It was the weird guy who had gotten me fired from my job the day before. Only this time, there was something black scrawled across his forehead. I gasped when I realized something even more bizarre...

My initials were written on his forehead with a black marker.

Chapter 2

I had to call the law, after all.

I wondered, *how should I report that I found the dead body of a stranger who just got me fired, especially when my initials are written right on his forehead?*

It was a tough decision, but I figured it was better to call than not. I took a few minutes to calm down, and pulled my phone out of my back pocket. My hands were still shaking when I dialed 911.

I decided to only mention the dead body and keep the rest of the information to myself for now. The authorities just needed to know the basics, as far as I was concerned. I needed some time to figure this mess out, and didn't want to be falsely accused of anything I would never do.

It took about a half hour for the sheriff's deputy to arrive from out in the county. I passed the time and eased my mind by throwing a tennis ball for Chevy out in the field. A tennis ball always kept my dog occupied for hours. We were in the middle of a game of fetch when Deputy Donaldson pulled up. He was known by the locals as Deputy Don.

"So, if it's not the Butterfly Boy." Don chuckled as he got out of his squad car.

Chevy recognized him, ran over and forced the slobbery wet tennis ball into the deputy's hand.

"Sorry, Chevy, duty calls. Not the best time for fetch." Deputy Don said, as he put on a pair of sunglasses with his free hand.

I took the tennis ball from the deputy and tossed it out in the field for Chevy. As he raced after it, I pointed the officer in the direction of the body.

*****

Chevy was affectionately known as Butterfly Boy by most of the search and rescue team personnel in our area. This included Deputy Don Donaldson, since he was also a volunteer cadaver dog handler for the local SAR team. I volunteered as a dog trainer.

The wilderness SAR dogs worked any hour of the day or night to find missing persons lost in the outdoors. That included weather like rain, sleet or snow. These dogs excelled in finding lost people and victims who died under all types of conditions.

Chevy on the other hand, excelled at playing fetch and making friends. He just didn't have the drive to focus on a work assignment. One day, I took Chevy out to a team training and tested his potential search and rescue abilities. He spent the whole time playing with butterflies, much to the delight of the hard core search and rescue crowd. The name "Butterfly Boy" was born.

It was okay. I loved Chevy for who he was created to be, and he was not meant to be a working dog. He was my best hiking buddy and a friend to animals everywhere. He was a happy momma's boy, and that was fine with me.

Search and rescue work was my passion, even though it was strictly volunteer work. It allowed me to combine my love of dogs and nature, and help people in the process. I jumped into the work wholeheartedly when I moved to the mountains several years ago.

My role in search and rescue had evolved in the past ten years, from dog handler to trainer. I now focused on helping other volunteers get themselves and their dogs ready for search and rescue missions.

Today's hike with Chevy had turned into a body recovery mission that I wanted no part of.

Chapter 3

Deputy Don walked over and said, "He's dead all right, a day or less if I'm guessing.

I nodded. "I would guess about the same."

"I don't think he is from around here," was the best answer I could come up with.

"There's no weapon and there are no fresh tire tracks coming in here from the road," Don noticed. "No one has driven through the mud since the rain last night."

A strange chill ran up my spine as I watched the deputy write in his notebook.

"Wonder who wrote A.M.B. on his forehead. Did you see anyone else out here today?" He was full of questions.

Since I was stuck in this conversation, I told him that Jase and his boys had been bothering Miss Judy and how I' been checking up on her and found her upset. I told him about taking Chevy for a walk to investigate and then coming across the body and calling the authorities.

"It's been a crazy day," I finished, still not believing how my day had ended up.

He asked some more basic questions and after a half hour of questioning, I was free to leave. I breathed a sigh of relief. Nothing he had asked required me to lie.

I walked down the paved road back to Miss Judy's house as fast as I could go. Chevy easily kept up, carrying his slimy tennis ball with pride. When we reached Miss Judy's house I headed straight to my truck.

"Chevy, Load."

Chevy jumped right into the back of the truck. "Load" was the only command Chevy always obeyed – mainly because he loved riding in the truck. I had a camper shell installed on the bed of my truck so he could ride safely in the back and have a place to stretch out and rest. It had sliding windows with screens on the side for nice air flow in good weather.

Actually, the camper shell also helped keep the windows clean in the cab of my truck. Chevy loved to lick windows, and he constantly left slobbery lick marks all over the glass. At least this way the lick marks stayed on the windows in the back of the truck.

I jumped in my truck and stepped on the gas. I would talk to Miss Judy about her beloved deer and Jase Johnson later. Besides, I was sure that the deputies would be up here to talk to her about the dead man before long.

It would only be a matter of time before Deputy Don found out that this dead stranger - whoever he was – had gotten me fired yesterday. I had enough problems and did not want 'murder suspect' added to the list.

I needed to find some information fast. There

was one place in town where I could acquire it, and I was on my way to get some answers

Chapter 4

It was almost five o'clock when I pulled up to Millie Ham's diner. Chevy barked with delight in the back of the truck and licked the camper shell windows as usual. At least one of us was having a great time.

The bells on the door jingled as I stepped into the country diner, announcing that another customer had arrived. The delicious smell of homemade biscuits filled the air, making me instantly hungry. I walked up to the counter and Miss Millie gave me a smile and a big hug.

"Avery, don't you worry about being fired. I would have saved those animals, too." Her soft blue eyes showed a motherly concern.

Boy, news sure travels fast in this town, and I just walked into information central.

"Thanks, Millie. I saw those dogs get hit by a car and just had to get them to the vet. I should have told someone before I left the office. But, Millie, my mind was in animal rescue mode and I didn't even think about it."

"Why didn't you fight to keep your job? Lots of people here would back you up, you know," Miss

Millie said.

"I don't know." I looked at her truly unable to answer the question. Why didn't I fight for my job? "The whole thing was stressful."

"You need to stand up for yourself more!"

"I've heard that before," I said with a short laugh. "Anyway, there are other jobs out there."

"Good for you," Millie bellowed. "But I still think the man that complained about you should get run out of town."

That gave me pause. She didn't know that the man had already run out of *life*.

Suddenly, there was a loud crash right outside the building, followed by the sick sound of metal scraping metal. I ran to the big picture window and saw that a pickup truck had run straight through the parking lot fence. Several feet of crumpled fence were scrunched up under the truck tires.

"PAPAW'S HERE! AND HE RUN RIGHT INTO THE FENCE THIS TIME!"

Millie Ham's five year old granddaughter, Abigal, was right about that. She was a tiny little thing, but had the loudest voice this side of the Smoky Mountains.

Miss Millie looked after Abigal during the day while the girl's mother worked at the grade school. She seemed like a pretty good kid, but she yelled everything she ever said. Not the best way to communicate, in my opinion.

Charlie Ham lumbered out of the truck, adjusted his worn-out ball cap and headed into the diner just like nothing had happened. He wore denim overalls and farmer boots, like most of the elderly men in our area.

The folks in the restaurant went right back to eating their meals.

Charlie's fender benders were considered normal around this town. They happened pretty much on a daily basis. I never figured out how he was able to keep his driver's license. Most folks called him Old Man Crash. I kept it more respectful and just called him Charlie – and I was glad to see him.

Charlie wasted no time updating everyone on the latest gossip.

"I heard they found a dead body out in Miss Judy's field this afternoon. They're trying to find out who he is and why he was in town."

Miss Millie said, "I wonder if it was that man who came in here the other day asking Charlie about Crazy Flora Jones."

That got my attention. "A stranger was in here asking about who?"

"Flora Jones. She moved here from up north about a month ago. She bought that old cabin up on Hatcher's Ridge. She's just plain crazy. "

"What's crazy about her?" I couldn't help but ask.

"She don't never talk to anyone. It just ain't normal, if you ask me. Bless her heart, she just stays up there on the ridge and never comes into town. Even sends her son to get groceries," Miss Mille said.

My body tensed. "What did the man look like?"

"Dark hair and a dark jacket," Charlie said and rubbed his eyes. "Can't tell you much else 'cause I wasn't wearing my glasses."

I've never seen Charlie ever wear his glasses, I thought.

Without asking, Miss Millie poured Charlie a cup of coffee and continued on without missing a beat. "Her son's name is Rick. He loves my banana cream pie. Sure is a handsome young man, with lots of muscles. I heard he goes to the bar to play pool with Jase Johnson and that crew."

My stomach turned when I heard Jase's name, and I forced myself to stay focused on the conversation.

Charlie added, "And he was flirtin' with your crazy friend, Jamie. You know how Jamie loves to look at all the guys wearin' jeans."

I laughed, imagining my best friend staring at some guy. "Yes, she does like a man in jeans."

Boy, the things Miss Millie and Charlie knew about. *I wonder what they say about me...*

One thing was for sure. The dead man couldn't be Flora's son Rick. The deceased looked over forty-years-old and definitely wasn't muscle bound.

My thoughts were interrupted by little Abigal's cries.

"PAPAW, JOE JOE'S HITTING ME! TELL JOE JOE TO STOP HITTING MEEEEEEE!"

Charlie bent down and said to Abigal's little brother, "Joe Joe, stop hitting Abigal."

"JOE JOE, STOP TOUCHING MEEEEE! MAMAW, JOE JOE'S TOUCHING ME!"

It was time for me to get out of there before that kid blew my eardrums out.

As I said good-bye, Miss Millie offered, "Give your sweet Chevy some of my homemade dog cookies."

She handed me a small paper bag stuffed full of doggie treats.

There was no use arguing with her, so I said "Thanks, Millie. Chevy will love them."

My dog was one of the most popular folks in town.

As I walked out to the truck, dog cookies in hand, I wondered if Rick was one of the guys I saw driving around with Jase earlier in the day. Did they hunt down more than just Miss Judy's deer this morning? And why?

Chapter 5

Jamie was not exactly the first person I would have chosen to do detective work, but she was my best lead. I picked up the phone and gave her a call.

"Hey, Jamie, I heard you met a new guy named Rick the other night."

Jamie squealed with delight. "Oh girl, he is a hunk-a man!"

In Jamie language, that meant he was strong, handsome and looked good in jeans.

I closed my eyes tight and said something I never wanted to say to Jamie. "Do you want to go out to the club tonight?"

"You KNOW IT! Let's party! Whoo Whoo!" She was ready to go. 24/7.

Jamie was always ready for fun, especially if there were guys around. She wasn't a tramp or anything like that. She just liked the attention that came with flirting. I needed to depend on her flirting skills to get more information that night. My flirting skills were zip.

I took a deep breath and said, "Okay, I'll meet you there around ten."

*****

The club, as I called it, was really just a small local bar with a couple of pool tables, a little area to dance, low lights and some music. That was all the folks around here wanted in a bar.

Jamie was leaning against the bar talking to a good-looking, muscular guy when I arrived. Her eyes sparkled and her shoulder length black hair bounced when she turned her head. It always made me smile the way her face lit up like a Christmas tree whenever a good looking guy was around.

She ran over to me and gave me a huge hug. "Wow, you look great." I rolled my eyes, my simple jeans and button up shirt was about as close to fashionable as I ever got. I did swipe on a little lip gloss and brushed my shoulder-length brown hair back from my face. In my twenties, I used to get dressed up all the time. Now, with thirty and a few years behind me, I honestly couldn't care less.

"Thanks, you look cute too." And she did. The turquoise top she wore highlighted her bright blue eyes.

Still smiling at the compliment, she leaned over and whispered, "That's Rick, the guy you were talking about. I told you he was a hunk! Come on, I'll introduce you."

She literally grabbed my arm and half drug me over to where her hunk-a man stood. I didn't even get a chance to tell her what was going on and why I wanted to meet her tonight. I decided to just roll with it. I needed to find out if this guy's momma knew the dead stranger from Miss Judy's field.

Jamie chirped, "Hey Rick, this is my friend Avery

– she's a dog lover, too."

I watched him closely for any signs of recognition. Nothing. His eyes only sparkled at the dog lover part. "Nice. What kind of dog have you got, Avery?"

"I have the best kind, a rescue." I added as I smiled into his brown eyes. A golden retriever mix, biggest, sweetest baby you've ever seen."

"Nice. My yellow lab died a few years back. Still miss him."

"Hey, don't I know you? Aren't you Flora's son?" I tried to be casual but realized I was holding my breath. "Actually, I need to talk to your mom. Would you mind getting me in contact with her?"

His eyes immediately darkened and his jaw clenched. Every muscle in his whole body tightened. He turned to walk away and hissed, "Don't you ever go near my mother."

Dang it, it's not like I'm a trained detective. *Guess I made my move too soon. Should have let him drink a few first.*

Things went downhill from there. I looked across the room through the dim lights and Rick's buddies glared at me like a pack of wolves.

"Nice job," Jamie said, rolling her eyes. "I think you now hold the world speed record for running guys off. Something like 3.5 seconds if I had to guess."

I asked her over the beats of the music on the jukebox, "Do you think you could keep Rick occupied for an hour or two? I'm going up to Hatcher's Ridge and try to find his mother."

"Sure, I'll dance with him all night if you want me

to. Why do you need to see his mom?"

"I'll tell you later, I promise. Think you can keep him here for a while?"

Jamie smiled and winked. "Yes, I promise to dance with him real s l o w.

As I headed out the door, I glanced over to see if Rick would even be willing to allow Jamie to be near him again. I should have known better, of course he did. Soon, my best friend was pulling him onto the dance floor.

Chapter 6

There are a couple unwritten rules in these mountains. You do not trespass. You do not go nosing around in the dark near a stranger's house. There are other rules, too, but those were the ones I hoped not to break. The consequences tend to be pretty bad.

Chevy was licking the back windows of the truck when I made it out to the club's parking lot. I hoped he would stay quiet for the five-mile ride up to Hatcher's Ridge. It would be hard to travel undercover with a dog barking with delight the entire way there.

I realized that ten thirty at night was not the best time to do this, but at least Jamie had Flora's son occupied. As I drove up the curvy mountain road toward the cabin, I noticed how the moon gave off a soft white glow and I was starting to enjoy the peaceful night.

I pondered what I would say if I got a chance to talk to Crazy Flora Jones. It was probably best to just relax and keep the conversation casual. My thoughts were abruptly shattered, when out of nowhere, bright floodlights filled my truck.

The harsh light virtually made it impossible to see the road in front of me. All I saw were two white lights bursting though the dark into my back window. The shouts of angry men took over the quiet night.

A sudden crack of gunfire filled the air, followed by a boom much closer. My steering wheel jerked to the right before I was able to control the direction. My smooth ride suddenly became a very bumpy one.

One of my tires had been shot out. The truck rolled to a stop, and within a few seconds, the passenger side window of my truck shattered. My heart hammered in my chest and fear spiraled throughout my nervous system.

I couldn't see anything but bright light. Then everything went dark.

*****

I slowly opened my eyes and found myself looking directly up at the clear night sky. The air smelled so fresh and clean, and the forest trees above me swayed softly in the breeze. My first thought was how beautiful the stars looked. That thought abruptly changed when I realized I was lying on my back in muddy water.

Where is my dog?

I slowly sat up and called out to Chevy, as I noticed three male figures huddled in the distance. A middle-aged lady sat silently on a log next to me, giving treats to my dog. Go figure. I was sprawled out in a mud puddle while Chevy had the time of his life. He made friends wherever he went. The lights of my truck illuminated the entire scene.

The woman said, "I'm Flora Jones. I hear you

wanted to talk to me."

"Yes, ma'am," I said. "Do you know who just tried to run me off the road?"

"That was my son, Ricky, and his friends. They're pretty protective of me. Isn't that sweet?" She sounded like a proud mother. "There's nothing for you to worry about. I raised my Ricky right and he would never hurt a woman."

Raised him right? This woman really must be crazy. "Then why am I lying in a mud puddle on a dirt road?"

The woman rolled her eyes, as if it was the silliest question ever asked. "You must've hit your head 'cause you passed out when they opened the door to your truck."

"I guess that would explain it." I pressed my hand to my forehead. Sure enough, there was a painful knot.

"The boys already put the spare tire on your truck," Flora said. "I don't think the flat tire is going to work anymore."

"Okay, thanks," was all I could muster up.

I wanted to avoid any further trouble and kept the conversation friendly. I guessed Jamie's tactic to slow dance with Rick didn't work out as planned. With no cell phone reception up in this mountain, Jamie wouldn't be able to warn me.

Flora said softly, "You have such a nice dog. When I saw him, I knew you must be a good person. I love his soft golden fur and happy personality. What was it you wanted to talk to me about?"

She spoke to me, but kept her focus on feeding dog cookies to Chevy.

As I sat in the mud, I told Flora the basic events of the past couple of days. I left out the part about my initials written on the dead guy's forehead. "I heard there was a stranger in town asking about you and wondered if he was the same person I found in the field."

She replied, "If the person you speak of is dead, then I hope it is the one and the same person." She looked at me and calmly continued, "Yesterday morning about six o'clock, my ex-husband showed up here. He abused me for years and forced me into hiding. As bad as it might sound, it would actually be a relief to me if he wound up dead."

Wow.

"What was he wearing?" I asked, trying to keep my voice equally calm.

"Let's see, all I remember is a dark jacket with some sort of patch on it. Like a target from a shooting range."

"Sounds like the same jacket the guy in the field was wearing," I said. "What's his name?"

"Richard Mallory, but everyone calls him Sniper. He loved to shoot at targets. Ridiculous, if you ask me." She took a long breath and held Chevy to her for a moment. "He scared me half to death yesterday," her voice had gone soft, shaky. "I didn't even recognize him at first, with that long hair and scruffy beard. He said he was buying some land here to keep an eye on me. I slammed the door shut and locked it, then called my son. "

"He was scruffy?" I asked.

"Very scruffy," she confirmed. "I'm glad my son is so protective of me."

"Sounds like you have a great son," I said, but didn't come close to meaning it.

"I do. Thank you."

"Did he say what land he was looking at?" I asked, looking for any bit of lead I could get. So far, nothing made sense. Well, I take that back...Richard Mallory was hated, it's not a surprise he ended up dead. But why my initials? How was any of this connected to me?

"Nah, didn't give him a chance. He took off when I told him Ricky was on his way."

"Any idea where he would have taken off to?"

She shook her head. "I didn't care. Anywhere but here was fine with me."

I thanked Flora and got Chevy loaded into the truck. The cool breeze flowed freely through the cab where the window had been broken out. My glove compartment was open and had been rifled through, but I didn't notice anything missing. I wasn't going to complain about it. At least the guys swept most of the glass out.

I decided it was best to count my blessings and get out of here while I could. *What a weird day.* As Chevy and I headed back toward home, one thought stayed in my mind. *How does a scruffy stranger show up in a small town early in the morning – and end up dead in a field, clean shaven, by early afternoon?*

Chapter 7

The next morning, I wanted to get a jump start on the day. I had quite a list of things to accomplish. One, find a new job. Two, solve a murder before I became the lead suspect. Three, get my truck window fixed.

What's the best way to prioritize that kind of to-do list?

I started with solving a murder, because the other two things wouldn't matter if I was in jail. Well, maybe solving a murder was a bit overly confident. I could at least get enough information to keep any suspicions off me. Deputy Don was good at his job, and I figured it wouldn't take long for him to find out about my whacked-out connection with the deceased.

I drove into town, which housed one barber shop and two beauty salons. Sniper must have gotten a haircut and shave somewhere. Using an educated guess, I headed over to the barber shop to see if I could come up with some more information.

The town barber's nickname was actually Barber. I always found that kind of humorous. At least it made his name easy to remember.

I pulled up right in front of the historic storefront

and got Chevy out of the truck. My best bet was to take him inside with me. The door to the barber shop creaked as I opened it and stepped inside and a bunch of elderly men looked at me, their eyes wide in surprise.

In this town, ladies did not tread into the barber shop. It was the men's domain. I quickly announced that Chevy wanted to visit all his buddies, so all was okay. Chevy trotted up to the line of men that sat in chairs along the wall, and got a scratch on the head from each one.

I asked Barber if there was an out-of-towner in here yesterday.

"A guy was in here calling himself Sniper" he said the name with such sarcasm, the old timers laughed.

"He came in here for a shave and cut. Gave him the $15 special," Barber continued. "The nut job didn't even want to talk. Who comes in a barber shop and doesn't want to talk?"

One of the old timers piped up, "Yeah, he was strange."

"I've heard that about him before," I said. "Do you know anything about him?"

"Nope, just what I told you," Barber answered.

As I got ready to leave, I noticed that Chevy had disappeared. That usually means one thing when we're indoors. The 'garbage man' was at work. Chevy had a knack for sneaking away to the nearest garbage can and finding himself a treat.

"Chevy, where you at, buddy?"

He wandered around the corner with a beef jerky wrapper hanging out of his mouth. That meant there was a tipped over garbage can nearby. I grabbed the wrapper and gave him a dog treat from my pocket as a fair trade.

Chevy's personality had always been 90% love and 10% mischief. The 10% part had just kicked in.

"Chevy, were you digging in some trash again?" An old timer laughed.

"Sorry, Barber, I should have named him Trashy." I had to laugh, too.

I walked down the short hall into Barber's office and picked up the trash can. Thankfully, it was just papers. As I scooped up Chevy's mess from the floor, I noticed a business card for Mr. Richard Mallory. A man like Sniper had a business card?

I stuffed the card in my pocket and took a quick glance at the other papers. It looked like some sort of demand to purchase Barber's land. There were also a couple of pictures of moonshine stills and a picture of a couple holding a baby.

Barber owned a piece of land about a mile or so from the field where Sniper's body was found. There had been rumors for years that Barber brewed and sold illegal liquor out there, but around this town, moonshine was viewed as a perfectly legitimate home-based business.

Why would Barber lie about knowing Sniper?

I quickly stuffed the papers back in the trash can, said my good-byes and headed out the door, Chevy in tow.

Chapter 8

I tried to figure out the whole Barber and Sniper connection as I walked out to my truck. I didn't see Deputy Don before I heard his smooth, deep voice.

"Want to tell me about the day you got fired, Avery?" He sounded so masculine that I knew he was in his sheriff deputy mindset.

Oh boy, here we go, I thought.

I cleared my throat and said, "Hey, Don. A couple dogs got hit and I ran to help them. They needed a veterinarian and I forgot all about work at that moment."

"And?" His hands were on his hips and his eyebrow raised with the question. I was toast. He already knew the answer, so it was time to fess up.

I exhaled a long breath. "A guy complained about me and I got fired for it."

"You mean Richard Mallory complained and got you fired?" Don sounded very serious.

"Yeah, I guess so." I took a deep breath, suddenly feeling defeated.

"Anything else you want to tell me?"

I thought my best bet was to let him know about

the papers in Barber's garbage can. At least that would get him off my back for a little bit.

"I found Richard Mallory's business card in Barber's office." I handed him the business card and continued on. "There are some other papers in the garbage can that look like there was a disagreement about some land. You may want to take a look."

"Okay. I'll do that," Deputy Don said. "Do you want to tell me what happened to your truck window?"

"Someone broke it out." I lifted my chin, refusing to say more.

"Maybe you should stop playing wanna-be detective."

"Maybe so."

As I loaded Chevy in the back of the truck, Deputy Don asked, "By the way, Avery, what is your full name?"

"Avery Meadow Barks"

"Initials A.M.B.?"

I swallowed and nodded, meeting his eyes. "Yeah. Can I go now?"

*****

Deputy Don strolled into the barber shop to get a haircut and chat up the old timers for information.

While he was there, the deputy borrowed Barber's office to make a private phone call. That was his way to get a look inside the garbage can. The deputy bent over and dumped out the office trash, including the pictures and the demands to buy Barber's land.

As he picked up the papers, something else caught his eye in the pile ... the empty packaging for a black magic marker.

Chapter 9

I spent a couple days job hunting with no luck. The economy was pretty tight in the rural areas and the stress weighed on me. The extra expense to get my truck window fixed was not welcome. I was over at the glass company getting an estimate for the repair when my cell phone rang.

"Hey, it's Don. Can you come out and help me with a cadaver search?"

"You know I only train dogs now."

"I know, but my dog is the only one available and I would feel better if I had you there. Just meet me over at Miss Judy's field."

"The same field where I found the body?"

"Same one"

"I've got Chevy with me, but he can rest in the back of the truck, I guess."

My truck window repair would have to wait.

I was somewhat confused as to why Don wanted me to accompany him on this search. If he was suspicious of me, wouldn't he want to keep me away from the original crime scene? Or did he want to keep me close because he did suspect me?

Is this guy trying to mess with my head right now, or what?

Chevy barked with pure joy as I pulled up to Miss Judy's field. Don was already there with his SAR dog and a couple of sheriff's deputies. Don was off-duty and worked the SAR mission in a volunteer capacity. His dog, Ace, was trained to find the scent of deceased persons.

As I walked up to the group, Don reported the latest news. "We received an anonymous phone call about a truck driving around in this field last night. The caller also stated that someone pushed a wheelbarrow along the back woods line." Don lifted his chiseled arm and pointed toward the woods. "The caller sounded drunk, so it's probably a wild goose chase."

Don turned to me and continued, "The sheriff asked me to work my dog out here, just to cover all our bases. I thought you might want to help."

"Is Miss Judy freaking out about all this commotion on her land?" I was worried about her.

"She doesn't know exactly why we're here. I told her we were still investigating," said Don.

"Well, we might as well get started."

I walked back to the truck and grabbed my radio and hip pack. Chevy's bowl was filled with water so he would be fine for a while. As usual, Butterfly Boy was having a great time licking the truck windows.

I caught up to Don as he prepared his search dog to work. He gave Ace the command, "Find."

The black Labrador started searching for a human death scent. Ace's nose immediately caught some scent in the air and his muscles tensed like an athlete. He followed the cone of scent back and forth through the field in the direction of the far woods line. It was beautiful to watch the dog work through the tall grass, his shiny black coat glistening in the sunlight.

The cadaver dog eventually reached the back edge of the field. As he neared the trees, he picked up speed. Ace worked into the woods through a small clearing, ran about two hundred feet across the vast bed of old brown pine needles and stopped directly in front of five dead deer.

The dog turned and faced his handler, sat down with military-like precision and stared Don straight in the eye. It was an obvious "cadaver sit alert", right next to the pile of dead deer.

My mouth fell open and I folded my arms across my chest.

The chubby officer that accompanied us on the search broke out in a booming voice, "Ahhh haaa haaa! Don, you have a great cadaver dog, don't yaa! Old Ace did a textbook alert right at dead deer! Haaa haaa"

Don stared at his dog and was at a loss for words. He muttered, "I can't believe this."

The officer continued his badgering. "Hey Don, I'll buy him for fifty bucks from ya. I want to take him hunting with me 'cause he's good at finding dead deer! Haaw haww."

The officer doubled over and held his stomach and continued his raucous laughter. Eventually, he caught his breath and stumbled out of the woods, back toward the field, still laughing as he went.

Don's face had turned beet red. He wouldn't

even make eye contact me. He just stood there in shock and stared out into the woods.

Finally he spoke up. "I don't know what's wrong with my dog. You know how hard it's been around here to get these guys to trust our dogs. I'll never be able to live this one down at the sheriff's department. We've spent so much time..." his voice trailed off and a look of pain, shame and humiliation was all over his face. He looked up at me. "I'll have to retire Ace, nobody will trust him now. Unless you want to work him." He turned and began to walk out of the woods.

I didn't understand it either. A cadaver dog should never alert on dead animals. The scent of a dead animal is very different than that of a dead human, especially to the sensitive nose of a trained dog. We trained many hours to make sure his dog only followed the scent of human death on the "Find" command.

As I started to walk with him, my first instinct was to console him. But my analytical thoughts took over. *Something's just not right with this picture.*

Suddenly, the mantra that many search and rescue dog handlers live by sounded like an alarm in my mind, *TRUST YOUR DOG!*

I punched Don's arm and said, "Don, I have trained with you about a hundred times. Your dog worked this scent perfectly. Your dog is trained not to go to dead animals, he did a perfect alert. Trust your dog!"

He stopped and just stood there, staring at his feet.

I continued, "What is one of the first lessons of search and rescue dog work?" I opened my arms in front of me. "TRUST YOUR DOG! If you're not going to do that, then I will."

I grabbed the radio from my pack and called the scene's incident command team. "Dog Team 1 to Command."

They answered back, "Command."

I reported, "Request assistance regarding a possible D-400."

D-400 was their code for deceased individual.

There was a long silence. I figured the deputy must have already reported in about the dead deer.

Finally, a voice came over the radio. "Affirmative. ETA ten minutes."

Don looked like he was about to hyperventilate. He grabbed the radio away from me and said a few curse words. Then he added, "Are you out of your mind?"

He paced back and forth in the woods, kicking up leaves and twigs.

Five minutes later, a bunch of law enforcement vehicles drove through the field and parked at the woods line. The deputy must have told them exactly where we were. The sheriff himself showed up, thanks to the rumor of the dead deer, and brought his entire posse into the woods to meet us.

Don's face turned white as a ghost, his dog and his entire training was on the line. He had worked so hard to bring search and rescue to this part of North Carolina. I hated to see him have such doubts.

I marched straight up to the sheriff and said, "This dog is well-trained and had a solid alert. I highly suggest you take it seriously." I put my hands on my hips. "Get some shovels over here and dig!"

The sheriff narrowed his eyes at me, clearly not used to taking orders. I held my ground and my faith in the dog we worked so hard to train. Finally, the sheriff ordered two of his deputies to get some shovels. He towered over me and calmly responded, "Might as well check it out. We're already out here."

I looked over at Don, who looked like he needed oxygen at this point. He headed out of the woods, with Ace in tow. His reputation with the sheriff was really on the line at this point, and he had lost all confidence in his dog.

I stayed in the woods and watched as the deputies removed all the deer from the pile. I felt the sheriff's eyes on me as his men pushed the shovels into the ground and removed the first clumps of dirt. My eyes remained focused on the ground where Ace had given his alert.

The deputies dug about a foot down, when a piece of blue and white cloth poked out from the earth below. The sheriff stepped forward, "Go easy, boys."

One of the men scraped the dirt away inch by inch, until a human arm appeared.

The sheriff nodded toward the hole, "There it is."

My heart started to beat rapidly. I was proud of Ace. He was right. There was a human body buried underneath all of those deer. I trotted out of the woods to find Don.

As I scampered across the field toward my truck, a voice echoed from the deputies' radios.

"D-400 confirmed. Be advised, it's Barber Pierce."

Chapter 10

The color quickly returned to Don's face when he heard the news. His dog had been right with the cadaver alert.

"Thanks, Avery. I owe you one." Don put his arm around my shoulders.

"No you don't, but you sure do owe Ace one," I laughed.

Ace trotted over for a scratch on the head when he heard his name mentioned.

Don took a step back and asked, "How did you know a body would be under there?"

"I've spent enough time training with you to know what your dog is capable of. It's also easier to trust the dog when you're not the handler," I said.

"I am just glad you believed my dog. " Don was ecstatic.

"I believe in you, too. Let's get to the trucks so I can check on Chevy."

Don was so relieved that his dog had been right that he hadn't yet focused on what it might mean to the investigation. I wanted to leave the area before he got back into his deputy investigative mindset.

At some point, he would wonder if there was a connection between my visit with Barber and his death. Maybe Don was already thinking about that. After all, I was the one who made sure that they dug where Ace had indicated.

I let Chevy out of my truck to take a quick potty break before we left. He bolted out of the truck and into the field. He was sniffing for the best spot to do his business over by the tree line when Old Man Crash arrived on the scene.

Charlie's truck bounced through the field right toward us. He didn't even attempt to slow down and ran directly into the back of my truck. The sound of twisting metal once again notified the world that Old Man Crash was in the area.

I closed my eyes, unable to believe it. *Great, now I have a broken window and a smashed up bumper.*

Charlie slapped his truck in reverse and sped backwards, slammed on the brakes, rolled out of his seat and said, "Avery, the tail lights on your truck aren't working."

Evidently he didn't realize that my truck was parked.

Don shook his head and piped in, "Charlie, her tail lights aren't working because you just broke 'em! I'm going to have to write you up a ticket for this one."

"Avery, I came to warn you." Charlie ignored both Don's comments and my bumper damage as he ambled toward us. "Jase Johnson was in the diner telling everyone that you might be the next one they find out in this field."

A shiver went up my spine. "Why would Jase say

something like that?" I wondered out loud. My stomach twisted at the thought.

Charlie went on, "He don't like you messin' up his deer huntin'. Miss Millie was worried when she heard they was a lookin' for another dead body out here and she made me come out here and find you."

Boy, the news sure travels fast around this town.

"Thanks, Charlie. Be sure to tell Miss Millie that I'm fine. "

"Yeah, I just heard that it was Barber's body that they done found." Charlie got town gossip faster than the cable news networks.

"JOE JOE, STOP TOUCHING MEEEEE! PAPAW, JOE JOE'S TOUCHING ME!" Little Abigal's hair fell in her face as she crawled out of Charlie's truck with Joe Joe following behind her.

"HI, OFFICERS! BARBER GOT KILLED!"

She continued her shouting. "JOE JOE PROBABLY KILLED HIM FOR GIVING HIM SUCH A STUPID LOOKING HAIRCUT!"

Charlie picked her up and said, "Hush, Abigal."

It was too late. Joe Joe already got revenge by finding a stick and poking Abigal.

"PAPAW, JOE JOE'S POKING ME! TELL JOE JOE TO STOP POKING MEEEEEE!"

Geez, no wonder Charlie's hearing went bad. This kid's voice was deafening.

Charlie lifted the kids back in his truck and cranked up the engine.

Little Abigal stuck her head out the window and yelled, "HEY, OFFICERS, WE'RE GOING TO HIGH HORSE FARM! PAPAW IS TAKING ME TO RIDE A

PONY!"

Joe Joe spoke up,"Abigal's face looks like a pony."

The young girl turned and put her hand over her little brother's mouth. At that point a mini wrestling match broke out between the two kids. I was relieved to see them buckle up.

Charlie hit the gas and bounced back out of the field toward the road. As they made their exit, Abigal's voice easily drowned out the sound of the engine,

"PAPAW, JOE JOE IS TOUCHING MEEEEEE!"

"Is it a good idea for him to have kids in the truck?" I asked Don, wincing as the truck pulled onto the road without stopping.

"No, not one bit," Don said, shaking his head. "I'll talk to him again later when I officially write him up. Luckily he can keep it between the lines. It's just his parking that stinks."

I watched until the truck was out of sight. "I hope he listens to you this time." I sighed and headed to look at the damage.

Chapter 11

The next morning came with a beautiful sunrise over the mountains. I was up early, thanks to all the stressful incidents running through my mind. I decided to take advantage of the beautiful weather and go on a little hike with my best buddy, Chevy. We both deserved some time to relax and enjoy nature.

As we drove down the side roads toward the state park, the fresh morning air flowed through the open windows. I grabbed my cell phone from my cup holder and called Jamie. Her laughter has always been a great remedy for stress, and I wanted to invite her on the hike.

Her phone rang several times but there was no answer. I made a mental note to try and call her again after we got back home this evening. I dropped the phone back in its place.

As I drove, my mind couldn't escape from the chain of events that had haunted my sleep. *Why were my initials on a dead guy's forehead? Does this whole thing even relate to me at all? What does Deputy Donaldson believe about it? Am I a suspect? How am I going to find a job? How long will my savings hold out? When can I get my truck fixed?*

And the biggest question of all...*why was Jase Johnson threatening my life?*

I needed to find a new source of income. I needed to make sure I didn't become a murder suspect. I needed to get my truck fixed, thanks to Rick's buddies and Charlie. But today I wanted to spend some quality time with my dog in the woods.

I eased into the small dirt trailhead parking area, got Chevy out and snapped on his leash. He jumped up and down with excitement, and wore his best doggy smile as we headed into the forest.

We hiked along our favorite trail for about an hour when Chevy stopped to splash in the nice cool creek. I rested on a rock and relaxed as he played in the water. Before long, a group of little kids came walking along the trail with a park ranger.

Most of the children walked closely together in single file. One little boy broke the mold and ran up and down the path. He suddenly stopped and stomped on a pile of old horse manure on the edge of the trail, sending small pieces of horse apples into the air. Horses used this trail once in a while, and they definitely were not potty trained.

The boy was amazed by a bunch of butterflies landing on the pile of horse manure. He giggled as he ran in circles around the piles and butterflies. I didn't know if he was more interested in the manure or the butterflies. Either way, it gave me a much needed laugh. I knew that Chevy would be very interested in the butterflies, so I kept him close to me.

The park ranger turned the boy's curiosity into an interactive class lesson. "Did you know that those purple butterflies are called Blues? The boy butterflies like to eat the horse poop to get nutrients, but the lady butterflies do not like to eat it. So, all those butterflies on the horse poop are guys!"

The little boy loved that idea. He laughed and said, "The park ranger said poop!"

All the little kids giggled and the girls pretended to be grossed out. The ranger smiled and got the group moving down the trail in single file again. The little boy skipped ahead of the group singing, "Ranger said poop, ranger said poop."

Chevy finished swimming and we strolled back down the trail to the parking area. As I loaded my wet dog into the back of the truck, it hit me like a ton of bricks....

"Let's go Chevy, I need to check something out."

Chapter 12

I reached Miss Judy's land, put the truck into four-wheel drive and hit the gas. My truck easily bounded across the mounds of grass and dirt, and we made it out to the back corner of her field in no time.

I jumped out and opened the tailgate. Chevy brushed past me as he dove to the ground, his soaked fur getting my t-shirt wet. As he romped through the tall grass, I started a search for horse poop.

I thought back to the day I found Sniper's body in the front of this field and remembered that Chevy played with a bunch of purple butterflies right in this area. I wondered if it was the type of Blues butterfly that the ranger had just spoken about.

My eyes scanned the ground as I marched back and forth through the tall grass, looking for a natural treasure. Five minutes into my search, I hit the jackpot.

"Yes! Horse poop!" I'd never been so happy to find a big pile of dung.

It was evidence that horses had been in this field recently. That might explain why there were no tire marks down near the road, and Sniper, or his killer, may have gotten here by horseback. It appeared that the law enforcement investigation focused on the road entrance to the field. This opened up a lot of new possibilities.

But how would a horse get back here?

I stood silently in the field, taking my time to look at every gap in the tree line. My dog let out a playful bark and I glanced up, but didn't see him.

I called, "Chevy!"

He sprinted out of a patch of woods, then made a U-turn and ran back the way he came. Curious about anything at this point, I jogged over to see what he was doing.

Behind an old abandoned shed I saw an opening in the woods. Once I stepped into the opening, it allowed me to see a grown over trail that continued out past the boundary of Miss Judy's property. It was several feet wide, and Chevy was jumping around with glee about two-hundred feet down the trail.

I hurried over and found him playing with more purple butterflies. There was another pile of horse manure close by.

Someone was riding horses through here for sure!

My best bet was to follow the horse trail. It might be a good lead for the authorities. Something inside me told me to grab my daypack before taking off on this hike into the unknown. I jogged back to the truck and put some extra water and supplies in the small pack before slinging it on my back.

Chevy and I were headed out for a walk on the mystery trail. Long tree branches reached out above the trail, creating a canopy of leaves and Chevy's golden hair bounced along in rhythm to his stride, as he enjoyed this new adventure. I just hoped I wouldn't get whacked by whoever owned the property.

We followed the meandering trail through the woods for about a half mile, when a familiar voice echoed from a distance.

"PAPAW, JOE JOE IS GETTING ON THE BROWN PONY! I WANT TO RIDE THE BROWN PONY!"

We followed another hundred yards down the trail, and the sounds of little Abigal grew louder and louder.

"PAPAW!"

Boy, I never thought I would be happy to hear that kid's voice.

Sure enough, the trail ended right on the edge of a horse farm. I could see the kids off in the distance riding ponies in a small fenced in area on the far side of the stables. I must've made it to the horse farm Abigal had talked about.

High Horse Farm was owned by none other than Barber Pierce. It was a five hundred acre farm that offered inexpensive boarding for horses and gave weekly riding lessons to the local kids in the front corral.

It was rumored that the real source of income for the farm was a moonshine still hidden in the back section of the property. Barber's son, Lucky, ran the place and was known to be one of the most skilled moonshiners in the region. Lucky was also one of Jase Johnson's buddies.

Even though bootlegging was an accepted

practice in the area, it was still against the law and could potentially land someone in jail. Therefore, he was very strict about the back section of their property.

Lucky didn't want anyone trespassing on his land, and that included dogs.

Chapter 13

I had a bad feeling in the pit of my stomach, and wanted to get Chevy on his leash and go back the way we came. I didn't want to give Lucky Pierce any surprises.

I called quietly, "Chevy." He didn't come.

I raised my right hand to my brow and looked in every direction but didn't see him. I stood quietly and listened, but only heard the leaves rustling in the breeze.

Adrenaline pumped through my body as panic reared up in every part of me.

"Chevy!"

My heart pounded in my chest and I struggled to breathe normally.

A soft creaking noise alerted me to a wide open door in an old barn close by. I hoped Chevy followed a fun smell or met a new animal friend inside. Maybe he was just distracted with a new buddy.

I walked softly, inching my way into the old barn, the door blowing shut behind me. I blinked, trying to adjust my eyes to the dim surroundings. Gradually, I noticed a couple vehicles and some old farm equipment stored in the barn, along with a lot of dirt and spider webs.

My hand groped for the flashlight in my pack, finally getting a good grip and pushing the rubber button to turn it on. As I scanned the light back and forth across the barn, I sensed some slight movements off to my right.

"Chevy?"

I lifted my arm and directed the light toward the movement. I jumped when I saw a tongue licking the windows inside a black car.

"Chevy? "

"CHEVY!"

I ran to every door on that car and pulled with all my strength. Nothing budged until I reached the back driver's side door. As I yanked on the door, it flew open and Chevy bounced out, ready to play. I dropped to my knees and gave him a big hug and a kiss on his forehead.

Chevy licked my face, then turned around and jumped back in the car. He jumped in, then out, then in, then out. This was weird behavior that I hadn't seen in him before. As I watched him jump in and out, I noticed that this car was not nearly as dusty as the other stuff in the barn.

I moved the light across the length of the car and got a small reflection back. I took a step closer and a design became clear on the side window. It was a sticker of a bulls-eye symbol.

This must be Sniper's car!

I bent over and poked my head inside the car door, flashing my light inside. The bright beam landed directly on a pale face with big eyes staring right back at me!

I jumped back with a start and smacked my head on the door panel. Rubbing my head and squinting, I recognized a familiar face.

"Jamie?"

Strands of black hair hung across her face and her eyes were wide with fright. Duct tape covered her mouth and was wrapped around her hands and feet. I reached up to push the hair off of her face and was stunned when I noticed A.M.B. written on her forehead.

I grabbed my phone from my pack and called Deputy Don's number.

He answered the phone on the first ring, "Hey Avery, what's up?"

"High Hor..."

CLICK

Someone ripped the phone right out of my hand.

Chapter 14

Lucky Pierce stepped out from the shadows behind me. His hair was disheveled and his clothes were filthy. He was irate and looked insane. And he had a gun.

"So, if it ain't the nature girl herself. What 'cha doing trespassing on my property?"

I turned the light toward his eyes and tried to sound brave.

"Why are my dog and friend locked up in a dead man's car?"

He reached over and grabbed the flashlight out of my hand. Lucky smelled as bad as he looked. I hoped he had not noticed how bad my knees were shaking.

He stalked over to the car and rummaged through the trunk, grumbling, "You nut cases are on my last nerve." The gun pointed in my direction.

I assumed he was searching for some rope to tie me up, but I lost my breath when he pulled out an old gas can and some matches. Alarms rung in my head telling me to run, but there was no way I could leave my dog and friend behind.

My best bet was to try and distract him. "Did you

kill Sniper?"

He snorted. "No, I did not, Little Miss Nosey."

I took a deep breath and said, "I think you killed him because he was blackmailing you about your moonshining."

He stepped toward me and stuck his chest out. Was that pride I was seeing? "My daddy killed him. Self-defense. Sniper stole Daddy's woman and baby thirty years ago. Now he tried to steal his land."

"You mean Barber had another kid?" Now, I was really confused.

"Yea, I just found out I have a brother. Never even got to grow up with him." Lucky shook his head sadly, "I always wanted a brother and Sniper took him from me before I was even born."

Lucky tried to hold back tears, but a few found their way down his face anyway. He was angry, emotionally overwhelmed and crazy. This wasn't good at all.

He continued on, "We threw his body on the back of my horse and I dumped him out in a field. I stood right over him and wrote on his head. I Avenged My Brother."

A.M.B. meant 'avenged my brother'?

Lucky looked exhausted, like he hadn't slept or bathed since the incident took place. There were deep circles under his eyes and his hands shook in an endless tremor.

I decided to keep pressing him. "Did you avenge your brother by also killing your daddy? How's hurting Jamie going to avenge your brother? What's with all these crazy initials on everybody's head?"

Lucky stomped the dirt and marched back and

forth, waving his arms in the air. He stopped, suddenly calmed and calculated, "You ain't figured it out yet? You're gettin' set up, you dingbat!" He reached into his back pocket and pulled out some type of paper.

"I got your truck registration right here, and A.M.B. is your initials. You sure ain't in the genius club!" Lucky spat on the dirt floor and crammed my truck registration back in his pants.

They did take something from my truck up at Hatcher's Ridge after all. To set me up?

Think. Think. I decided to try and distract him some more and mustered up some attitude. "Lucky, why did you kill Barber?"

He pounded his fist on the hood of the car and sobbed. "I would never hurt my daddy. The stress killed him and he just keeled over and died. Jase helped me bury him."

"May he rest in peace." I tried to roll with it, but Lucky only stared at me, his jaw clenching in fury. "Why did you bury your daddy under a bunch of deer carcasses?"

"He liked huntin'!" Lucky sounded exasperated, like I already should know the answer.

"That makes sense," I lied.

"That makes sense," he mimicked in a feminine tone. "Here's what makes sense."

Without a word, he stuffed the gun in his pants and grabbed the gas can and matches, and walked out the door. I heard the sound of heavy chains and locks on the other side. A soft glow rose from the trunk of the car and I realized he left my flashlight behind. I reached for it, thankful to not be in the dark.

I jumped when Lucky hollered through the door, "Don't even think about yellin' out for help. If I hear ya, I'll have to hurt ya."

I guess I pushed him too far. Maybe I needed to brush up on my people skills.

I ducked back into Sniper's car and pulled the tape off Jamie's mouth. My hands shook so much that the tape didn't come off evenly. I tugged on it a few times and it finally peeled off her face.

"Owww," she cried out as she rubbed her mouth. Chevy jumped on top of her and licked her face. She hugged the dog to her, sobbing, "Thanks, Avery. Thanks, Chevy!"

"How'd you get in here, Jamie? What happened"

Jamie's eyes grew wide. "Rick took me out on a real date last night. Avery, I was so excited. I thought he really liked me." Tears filled her eyes. "We were down at the club and Lucky called Rick and asked him to stop by."

"It's okay," I said, pushing her hair from her face and wiping her tears. "Where's Rick now?"

She shook her head. "When we got out here, Lucky started on a rant, saying that Rick is really his brother. Rick didn't believe a word of it. They yelled at each other."

Ice pooled in my veins. "What did Lucky do?" I asked, afraid we'd find another dead body in the field. I didn't like Rick, but no mother deserved to bury her child.

"Lucky told Rick if he didn't believe it to just go ask his mama. I guess Barber and Rick's mama had a fling back in the day." Jamie shuddered and I patted her arm. "Rick freaked out and ran to find out from his mother."

"Rick left you with Lucky alone?" Anger rose in me at the thought of it.

Jamie stared at her hands and she let out a sad sigh.

"I'm sure he never imagined Lucky would do something like this. Maybe he came back and couldn't find me," she said softly. It sounded like she was trying to convince herself of that unlikely possibility.

Suddenly, Chevy bolted out of Sniper's car and landed on the dirt floor. His nose bobbed in the air and he started whining. It took a full minute for me to realize why.

I smelled smoke.

Chapter 15

I beat on the wooden door and pushed with every ounce of energy I had. The locked chains clanked together with each shove. The door wouldn't budge, but my escape attempt made Lucky furious.

"You're gonna get it now!" he yelled through the door, rage living in his words.

"Lucky, I'm sorry," I yelled back. "Please don't do this. Let us out."

Nothing. Was he gone? I didn't hear any more out of Lucky, but my heart raced when I heard the crackling of the fire. Smoke started to enter the barn through the cracks in the wood walls. I knew that smoke inhalation killed before a fire consumes a building. We needed to get out of there fast.

I searched the walls of the barn, looking for loose boards or a secret door. Jamie was screaming from the back of the car. I ran back to her, planning to untie her so she could help when Chevy bounded up to me, shaking his head back and forth. There were car keys in his mouth and he wanted to go for a joy ride. "Chevy, smart dog!"

I grabbed the keys out of his mouth, and jumped

in the driver's seat of Sniper's car. Jamie was still tied up in the back seat and sounded like she was hyperventilating.

I gave Chevy his favorite command. "Chevy, Load."

I said a little prayer and put the key into the ignition. The car cranked up just as the smoke was packing down on us.

I yelled to my passengers, "Hang on, we're going 'Old Man Crash' on this situation!"

I squeezed my eyes shut and stomped the gas pedal to the floor. The car flew forward and we headed straight for the old rickety wall, crashing through and bursting out the other side. Wood and debris flew everywhere as we knocked over a fence and drove through some bushes. I finally opened my eyes and let off the gas. As we rolled to a stop in a horse pasture, Chevy was barked with delight.

I looked in the rear view mirror as the barn went up in flames. I opened the car door and jumped out as a bunch of sheriff deputies sped through farm's front gate. I reached into the car and honked the horn as they raced across the property, relief causing my knees to go weak.

Deputy Don roared in with lights flashing and parked about ten feet away. He ran toward me, radioing for the fire department to respond as a sheriff's K9 went crazy and went running toward the woods.

"He has a gun," I warned and said a prayer that everyone would be safe.

They found Lucky Pierce hiding, and he was soon handcuffed and shoved into the car. I saw the deputy wrinkle his nose and I felt sorry for him having to ride in close quarters with the horrible smelling man.

While all that was happening, a young, good looking deputy pulled Jamie from the car and cut the duct tape from her hands and feet. She looked over at me with a great big smile and winked. Her attention quickly returned to flirting with the deputy.

"At least she picked a law abiding guy this time," I laughed to Don and then grew serious. "How'd you know to come here?" I was surprised to see such a show of force.

"It was a shot in the dark. I heard you scream 'High Hor' on the phone before it went dead. The kids talked about High Horse Farm, and add to that Sniper's attempt to blackmail the owners of this farm. I figured there may be some trouble out this way."

I leaned against the car, my legs still a little wobbly. "Thank you."

"I'm just glad you are all okay."

Chevy barked and drew my attention. He ran across the pasture toward a group of butterflies.

I smiled. Everything was okay now.

Chapter 16

Exactly a week later, there was a big celebration out at Miss Judy's field. The town folk decided to make the field a positive place and held a mini-county festival.

The high school band played and there was a big cook-out. The local ladies brought all kinds of pies and desserts, and the local dogs came out to play with Chevy.

The sheriff walked up the stairs onto a makeshift podium and called Chevy to come up in front of the crowd. I accompanied him and stood in front of the sheriff and Deputy Donaldson.

"Chevy, you have helped this community due to your bravery," Deputy Donaldson said, taking the microphone first.

The sheriff piped in," I present you with the award 'Honorary Sheriff Detective Dog, in charge of Community Relations'."

Deputy Don gave a little plaque to me in Chevy's honor while the crowd clapped and cheered. Then came the prize Chevy was most happy about – a new tennis ball – and the first throw for a game of fetch was by the sheriff himself.

Several volunteers from the gardening club planted butterfly bushes in the field just for Chevy. Miss Judy got up to say how much she loved Chevy and wanted him to have butterfly friends here all his life.

I was basking in the fun and the sunshine when Deputy Don walked up with a ruggedly handsome stranger.

"I want to introduce you to Rocky," Don said. "He just got a permit to build an animal sanctuary in the next county. He read about you and Chevy in the local paper."

Rocky went straight to the point. "Would you be interested in training dogs at our new animal sanctuary?"

"Wow," I began, so surprised I almost couldn't find words. "I'm honored you came all the way out here just to offer me a job."

He raked a hand through his hair and looked at me, his face growing serious. "Well, it's more than just a dog training job." His voice was rugged, too. "Some strange things have been happening on our land and I thought you and your dog could help us. Let's take a ride over there and I'll fill you in along the way..."

About The Author

Mary Hiker spent her childhood rescuing animals, playing in the outdoors and reading Nancy Drew Mysteries. Fast forward quite a few years and her books reflect the passions that started in her youth.

She now lives in the western North Carolina mountains and spends lots of time in the forest enjoying nature. Mary is a true animal lover and her own dogs are the inspiration behind Chevy's hijinks in the Avery Barks Dog Mysteries series.

You can visit Mary at her website and sign up for her Newsletter to be notified when new books are released.

www.maryhiker.com

Made in the USA
Middletown, DE
04 September 2023